Yaiya,
Where Are You?

K.L. WILLIAMS

To order additional copies of this book, contact:
Xlibris
1-888-795-4274
www.Xlibris.com
Orders@Xlibris.com

ISBN: Softcover   978-1-9845-8043-6
         EBook   978-1-9845-8042-9

Print information available on the last page

Rev. date: 05/22/2020

This book is dedicated to the memory of my late wife, Margarette Williams. Thank you, honey, for three decades of love, laughter, and the gift of four wonderful children who keeps giving. Life was so easy to live because you were so easy to love.

*K*elden stood at the top of the stairs and yelled, "Good morning, everybody!" Then he sat down and slid all the way down, one step at a time. Bump, bump, bump on his little rump. And when he hit the floor, Kelden sprang to his feet and sprinted to his grandma's bedroom door.

"Yaiya, it's me, Kelden. Can I come in? I have something to tell you." But there was no reply to his cry.

Kelden knocked on the bedroom door and yelled, "Yaiya, it's me, Kelden. I have something to tell you. Are you in there?" But again, there was no reply to Kelden's cry.

Kelden opened the door and stepped inside the room. He looked around for his *yaiya*, but she wasn't there. "Yaiya, where are you?" he screamed.

"Kelden, don't you remember? We talked about this just yesterday. Your yaiya has gone away, and she's not coming back," said Dylan, Kelden's dad.

"You mean, my yaiya is in heaven," Kelden responded hesitantly.

"Yes, Kelden, your yaiya is in heaven now, and that's where she's gone to stay," answered Dylan.

Kelden paused for a moment. He seemed a little confused by his father's answer. "Daddy, can I go to heaven to see my yaiya?" he asked.

"Yes, Kelden, one day you will go to heaven and see your yaiya, but not today. First you have to grow up, and you must be good. And when you are very old, you'll go to heaven too," explained Dylan.

Kelden sat down and started to pout. He folded his arms and lowered his head, and in a voice slightly above a whisper, he said, "I'm sad!"

"No!" shouted Kelden defiantly. "My yaiya is not in heaven. She's in her garden. She just told me so." Kelden jumped to his feet, and out the door he ran, dragging his father by the hand. When Kelden got to Yaiya's garden and saw that she wasn't there, he shouted, "Yaiya, where are you? You said you'd be here."

While Kelden and his dad stood at the edge of Yaiya's garden, a hummingbird flew by and took a few sips of nectar from the bird feeder that Yaiya had placed there to welcome her little friends to her garden. Next, the hummingbird flew over to Yaiya's treasured knockout rosebush plant and hovered there for a while.

"Ooh, Daddy, look, there's a hummingbird in my yaiya's garden," whispered Kelden.

The hummingbird hovered around each rosebush, inspecting each bud, enjoying their fragrance and their beauty too, just like Yaiya would do. And as if it spoke the magical word *open*, which only the rosebuds heard, they all unfolded at the request of the hummingbird.

*N*ext, the hummingbird flew over to Yaiya's giant sunflower tree and hovered in front of a huge bloom. I guess it was searching for a tasty treat, but then the hummingbird seemed to smile and blink an eye, staring at Kelden all the while.

"Daddy, that was awesome!" shouted Kelden. "Did you see that hummingbird just winked at me?"

The hummingbird dashed around Yaiya's garden with many chores to do, and when it was finished, off it flew, waving its wings bye-bye to Kelden.

"Kelden, I think we both can agree that your yaiya is not in her garden, now is she?" said Dylan.

"No, she's not," answered Kelden reluctantly. "But she could be in her gazebo. I'll go and see. Daddy, please come with me." And off he ran to the gazebo.

As Kelden drew closer to the gazebo, he started to doubt that his yaiya was in there, but he knew that the gazebo was the place she would go to escape the noonday sun when it got too hot for her to work in her garden. "Yaiya, it's me Kelden," he shouted. "I have something to tell you. Are you in there?" And then he waited for her to reply, but an answer never came to his cry.

Kelden opened the gazebo's door, and as he peeked inside, a butterfly flew by and brushed against his cheek. "Daddy, a butterfly just kissed me," he shouted excitedly. "But where did it go? Daddy, do you know?"

"Look, Kelden, it's over there." Dylan pointed. "Do you see it? The butterfly is in your yaiya's apple tree." Kelden looked in the direction his dad was pointing, and there right next to Yaiya's wind chime was the most magnificent butterfly he had ever seen.

"I see it. I see it, Daddy," cried Kelden enthusiastically. "My yaiya's butterfly is pretty."

*T*he butterfly flapped its wings and flew away, and as it rose slowly to the top of the apple tree, it vanished magically while Kelden waved bye-bye to the butterfly. And Yaiya's wind chime whispered a sweet melody in the slight breeze from the butterfly's wings.

"Kelden, now you know that your yaiya is not in her gazebo," said Dylan.

"I know, Daddy," replied Kelden sadly. "Perhaps she's in the RV with Marley and Mommy. Daddy let's go to the RV and see. Please come with me." And off they went to the RV.

*A*s Kelden climbed the two steps to the RV's door, he was confident that he had found his yaiya at last. "Yaiya," he shouted. "It's me, Kelden. I've got something to tell you. Please let me in." Then he waited patiently for his yaiya to open the door and let him in, but there was only silence from the inside of the RV. "Yaiya, I know you're in there. Why won't you answer me?" Kelden turned the latch on the RV's door to let himself in, but a dragonfly flew by and landed on him.

Kelden stared closely at the dragonfly on the back of his arm, as if there was something familiar he recognized about it. "Yaiya, come out and see the dragonfly that just landed on me. It looks like the one from your garden," he called happily.

The dragonfly rested there for a while, then off it flew, waving bye-bye to Kelden. "Daddy, Yaiya must not be in the RV," he said dejectedly. "She didn't come out to see the dragonfly that had landed on me."

Dylan looked at the sad face of his little boy and wondered how to help him understand what had happened to his yaiya. Dylan put his arms around his son and, as compassionately as he could he tried to explain, "Kelden, your yaiya is—"

"Daddy, please wait," Kelden interrupted. He knew what his dad was about to say, but he wasn't ready to accept the truth about his yaiya just yet. Besides, Kelden figured he still had one more place he could look to find his yaiya. "Daddy, my yaiya could be in my GP's den, asleep or watching TV. Please can we go and see." And without saying another word, they went back into the house.

*T*he door to GP's room was opened wide, so it was easy for Kelden to see inside. He saw a portrait of Yaiya on the mantle above the fireplace, her afghan blanket, her reading glasses, and her Bible lying on her reclining chair, as if she had just been there. But Yaiya wasn't anywhere. Frustrated and sad that he didn't find his yaiya in any of the usual places he thought she would be, Kelden muttered quietly, "Yaiya, where are you? I've looked for you everywhere. I was sure that you'd be in here."

*K*elden wandered into the living room where his GP sat in his chair, staring aimlessly out of the window. Kelden crawled up into his GP's lap and rested his head against GP's chest. "I'm not good at hide-and-seek," he said sadly. "I couldn't find my yaiya anywhere."

"Kelden, what did you want to tell your yaiya?" GP asked.

"*I* want to tell her that I love her," he said, and the tears rolled down his cheeks as he continued to speak. "My daddy said that she's in heaven now and that she's not coming back. I asked him if I could go to heaven to see her, but he said, 'Not today, not for a very long time.'"

"Kelden, your yaiya knows that you love her, and she loves you too. And someday, you'll get to tell her that for yourself," GP explained.

"GP, are you sad?" he asked.

"Yes, Kelden, I'm sad," GP answered.

"I'm sad too. My yaiya died," said Kelden. "But don't worry, GP. Yaiya is in heaven with Jesus."

"Yes, Kelden, she is in heaven with Jesus, and she's happy there. She's in no more pain, and she cries no more, and someday, we'll all meet her there," GP answered him.

"GP, I love you too," Kelden said.

"And I love you too, Kelden," GP replied. Then Kelden kissed his GP on the cheek, and they held each other and cried.

"Oh, GP, look. That's my friend Timmy. I want to play with him." Then Kelden jumped down from his GP's lap, and as he was headed out the door, he shouted, "See you later, GP."

"Hey, Timmy, wait for me!"

Lightning Source UK Ltd.
Milton Keynes UK
UKHW051300080620
364546UK00002B/61